Paddington
Goes to
Hospital

Action Medical Research and Paddington Bear

Paddington Bear has been at the heart of fundraising for Action Medical Research ever since his creator, Michael Bond, met the charity's founder, Duncan Guthrie, in 1976.

Paddington's cheery face has helped Action Medical Research attract thousands of new supporters, raising millions of pounds to treat sick babies and children in the UK and can often be found at fundraising events up and down the country.

Since 1952, Action Medical Research has spent more than £110 million on research that has helped save thousands of children's lives and changed many more. Its earliest research contributed to the development and rapid adoption of the first UK polio vaccines. Since then, it has supported further breakthroughs in medical care, including vaccines for rubella and Hib meningitis, the use of ultrasound scanning in pregnancy and awareness of the importance of taking folic acid during pregnancy to prevent spina bifida.

But there is still so much more to do. Paddington would love you to find out more about his favourite UK charity and how you can help, by visiting www.action.org.uk

action medical research
for children

First published in hardback in Great Britain by HarperCollins Publishers Ltd in 2001
First published in paperback by Collins Picture Books in 2002
Revised edition published in paperback by HarperCollins Children's Books in 2012
New edition published in 2015
This edition published as part of a set in 2017

1 3 5 7 9 10 8 6 4 2

ISBN: 978-0-00-796823-7

Collins Picture Books in an imprint of HarperCollins Publishers Ltd.
HarperCollins Children's Books is a division of HarperCollins Publishers Ltd.

Text copyright © Michael Bond and Karen Jankel 2001
Illustrations copyright © R. W. Alley 2001

Visit our website at www.harpercollins.co.uk

Printed in China

Michael Bond & Karen Jankel

Paddington
Goes to
Hospital

Illustrated by R. W. Alley

HarperCollins *Children's Books*

Paddington lay back on the lawn with his paws in the air and gazed up at the Browns. "Where am I?" he gasped.

"You're at home, dear," said Mrs Brown. "At number thirty-two, Windsor Gardens."

"Is that in Darkest Peru?" asked Paddington.

"If you ask me," said Mrs Bird, "that bear's lost his memory."

"Oh dear, Henry!" exclaimed Mrs Brown. "What shall we do?"

Mr Brown consulted his Medical Dictionary. "All it says here is, 'the victim shouldn't drive a car'."

"I don't think I could anyway," said Paddington. "I've hurt my shoulder."

"Would you like a bun?" suggested Mrs Brown.

"What's a bun?" asked Paddington.

"That settles it," said Mrs Bird.
"I'm phoning the hospital!"

"I'm sorry we took so long," said the ambulance driver. "When I heard the name 'Paddington' I went to the railway station by mistake. If you ask me," he added, "this young bear's not only lost his memory, he's put his shoulder out as well. One of you ladies had better come with him in case he has to stay in hospital overnight."

"Thank goodness I put his clean pyjamas out this morning," said Mrs Bird, trying to strike a cheerful note.

The ambulance crew soon made up for lost time, and with sirens wailing, Paddington reached the hospital in no time at all.

"Stand by for a young bear emergency," said the driver to the waiting staff, and with a count of three, they lifted Paddington on to a bed.

"Is it true that you've lost your memory?" asked a doctor.

"Would you mind repeating the question?" replied Paddington. "Phew! Phew!"

"I don't like the sound of his wheezes," said a nurse.

"I've think we've got complications," agreed the doctor. "He'd better go straight to x-ray."

"You've got complications!" exclaimed Paddington indignantly. "What about me? Phew! Phew!"

Paddington had never travelled anywhere on a bed before and he thought it was very good value. "There was nothing like this in Darkest Peru," he announced as they gathered speed. "Phew! Phew!"

When they reached the x-ray room, the lady in charge pushed
a large machine over the bed and made some adjustments.

"Now lie very still while I take some pictures," she said.
"Otherwise, they will come out blurred."

With that she went to the other side of the room, pressed a
button, and there was a whirring noise.

"Cheese!" said Paddington.

Afterwards, Paddington and Mrs Brown met the doctor again.

Paddington stared at the pictures on the wall. "What's happened to my fur?" he exclaimed. "I had it when I came in."

"It's still there," said the doctor. "This is a special camera for looking inside people – and bears, too," he added hastily.

"It looks very complicated," said Paddington. "I didn't know I had so much inside me."

"The one on the left shows why your shoulder's hurting," explained the doctor. "The bone's come out of its socket. We shall need to put you to sleep while we relocate it."

"Have you had anything to eat since breakfast?" asked a nurse.

"I haven't even had time for my elevenses," said Paddington.

"That's good," said the nurse,
wiping his arm with something cold.
"Otherwise you would have had to
wait while it settled."

Paddington felt a tiny prick,
and he was about to give the
nurse a hard stare…

…when his eyelids began to go droopy.

As soon as he was asleep the doctor turned to Mrs Brown. "We'll soon put things right. He won't feel a thing.

"As for his memory, it probably needs a jog, but a good night's rest often works wonders. I must say I'm a bit worried about his breathing, though."

"It's a mystery," said Mrs Brown. "He's never had this problem before."

Paddington woke to find himself in a strange room.

"Where am I?" he asked for the second time that day.

"You're in a ward with lots of other patients," said Mrs Brown. "And the doctor's put your arm back in its socket."

"I hope it's pointing the right way," said Paddington. "Otherwise, I shan't know whether I'm coming or going."

"I've brought you some water," said a nurse. "I expect you're feeling thirsty after your operation."

"I am," said Paddington.

He was about to ask for something more exciting to drink, but he couldn't think of the name.

"Tea?" suggested Mrs Brown.

"Bless you!" said Paddington.

"I expect they will keep you in overnight for observation," said Mrs Brown.

"I don't think I want anyone observing me asleep," said Paddington. "I might fall out of bed."

"Don't worry," said the nurse. "The sides lift up to stop that happening."

"Besides, I shan't be far away," said Mrs Brown.

At that moment Mr Brown arrived, carrying a bowl of fruit from all the traders in the market and a 'Get Well Soon' card from Paddington's friend, Mr Gruber.

"Even Mr Curry sent his best wishes," he said. "What it is to be popular."

The lady who brought Paddington's supper had been surprised to see him. "The boy who used to be in your bed liked his food hot and spicy," she warned. "I hope it's suitable for bears."

Paddington had told her not to worry.

"There's nothing wrong with your appetite," said a nurse, eyeing the empty plate.

"There is now!" gasped Paddington. And this time his 'phews!' sounded as though he really meant them, for he had never before tasted anything quite so hot.

"I think I'd better leave taking your temperature until you've cooled down," said the nurse. "I'll simply feel your pulse to be going on with."

Just then two more nurses came along pushing a trolley laden with bottles and jars.

"It's medicine time," said one of them, handing Paddington a small cup filled with pink liquid.

"I'd like another one of those, please," he announced. "I think it's doing me good already."

The nurse laughed. "I wish we had more patients like you."

When it was bedtime, Mrs Brown helped Paddington wash his whiskers and clean his teeth.

"If you need anything in the night," she said, "just press the emergency button and someone will come."

"Sleep tight," she said, lifting the sides on the bed.

"Oh, I shall," murmured Paddington. So much had happened to him he felt as though he might sleep for ever.

"I think," he announced to the world in general, "I might have an emergency button by my bed when I get home. I often want things in the night."

But he didn't have time to test the one in the hospital, for he was soon fast asleep.

Next morning, Paddington went for a walk round
the ward to meet the other patients.

One small boy had just
had his tonsils removed.

Another had fallen out
of a tree and broken his leg.

A girl had been rushed in to
have her appendix out.

Another boy had been knocked down by a car when he
ran across the road without looking.

Paddington decided he was really very lucky.

"You can always see people worse
off than yourself in a hospital,"
said a nurse.

"I can see why they're called
patients," said Paddington.
"Some of them must have
to wait a very long
time before they
get better."

To Paddington's surprise, when he got back to
his bed he found he had visitors.

Mr Brown held up an L-shaped piece of wood. "Do you recognise this?" he asked. "I found it when I was cutting the grass this morning."

"It's my boomerang!" exclaimed Paddington. "The one you gave me for my birthday. It's all coming back to me."

"Like it did yesterday morning!" said Mrs Bird. "Blessed thing! It must have flown back when you were testing it and hit you on the head."

"That's the trouble with boomerangs," said Jonathan. "They always come back."

"You'd better duck next time," agreed Judy.

"It's all your fault, Henry," said Mrs Brown. "No wonder Paddington lost his memory."

"Well, at least it seems to have been jogged back again," said Mr Brown defensively.

"Phew! Phew!" agreed Paddington.

"And that's another thing," said Mrs Bird. She held up a small silver object. "Guess what?"

"It's the present you gave me in case I ever have an emergency," said Paddington. "It must have fallen out of my pocket." He held the object up to his mouth and blew, "Phew! Phew!"

Several piercing blasts brought doctors and nurses running from all directions.

"It's nice to know it isn't broken. When I lost my memory, I forgot I needed a whistle to make my 'phews' work," said Paddington.

"All's well that ends well," said the doctor,
as the Browns explained what had happened.
"It's been a learning experience for us, too,"
he added, amid general agreement.
"It could come in very useful if we have any
more bear patients to look after."
"I'm glad you had me to practise on,"
said Paddington, as he waved goodbye.
"I've never been in a hospital before,
and now that I know what goes on,
I shall never mind
coming back!"

HOSP
QUI
PLEA

P.B.